STAND STRAIGHT, ELLA KATE

The True Story of a Real Giant

BY Kate Klise

PICTURES BY
M. Sarah Klise

DIAL BOOKS FOR YOUNG READERS
an imprint of Penguin Group (USA) Inc.

Sophia
Dream Big
2012

FOR DREAMERS, BIG AND SMALL

DIAL BOOKS FOR YOUNG READERS

A division of Penguin Young Readers Group / Published by The Penguin Group

Penguin Group (USA) Inc., 375 Hudson Street, New York, NY 10014, U.S.A.

Penguin Group (Canada), 90 Eglinton Avenue East, Suite 700, Toronto, Ontario, Canada M4P 2Y3 (a division of Pearson

Penguin Canada Inc.) / Penguin Books Ltd, 80 Strand, London WC2R 0RL, England / Penguin Ireland, 25 St.

Stephen's Green, Dublin 2, Ireland (a division of Penguin Books Ltd) / Penguin Group (Australia), 250 Camberwell

Road, Camberwell, Victoria 3124, Australia (a division of Pearson Australia Group Pty Ltd) / Penguin Books India

Pvt Ltd, 11 Community Centre, Panchsheel Park, New Delhi - 110 017, India / Penguin Group (NZ), 67 Apollo Drive,

Rosedale, North Shore 0632, New Zealand (a division of Pearson New Zealand Ltd) / Penguin Books (South Africa)

(Pty) Ltd, 24 Sturdee Avenue, Rosebank, Johannesburg 2196, South Africa / Penguin Books Ltd, Registered Offices :

80 Strand, London WC2R 0RL, England

The publisher does not have any control over and does not assume any responsibility for author or third-party websites
or their content.

Designed by Jennifer Kelly

Text set in Pabst L

Manufactured in China on acid-free paper

10 9 8 7 6 5 4

Klise, Kate.

Stand straight, Ella Kate : the true story of a real giant / by Kate Klise ; pictures by M. Sarah Klise.

p. cm.

Summary : A fictionalized biography of Ella Kate Ewing, born in 1872,

who was eight feet tall by the age of seventeen and who became financially independent by traveling the country for

nearly twenty years appearing at museums, exhibitions, and in circus shows.

ISBN 978-0-8037-3404-3

[1. Ewing, Ella Kate, 1872-1913—Juvenile fiction. 2. Ewing, Ella Kate, 1872-1913—Fiction. 3. Giants—Fiction.

4.People with disabilities—Fiction.] I. Klise, M. Sarah, ill. II. Title.

PZ7.K684 St 2010

[Fic]—dc22   2009033856

The illustrations in this book were done in acrylic on Bristol board.

Most tall tales are made up.
But my tall tale is true.
I was a giant—a real, live giant.

I wasn't born tall. I was a little baby just like any other born in 1872. Mama and Papa named me Ella Kate.

When I was still small, Papa went to the bank and borrowed
money to buy a farm in a place called Rainbow, Missouri. He built
a cabin from trees he cut with his own two hands.

We were a little family—just Mama, Papa, and me.

But I didn't stay little for long.

When I was seven, I started growing at a most startling rate.

Mama couldn't sew dresses fast enough to keep up. So she started adding fabric to the bottom of my favorite dress.

"Stand straight, Ella Kate," Mama said when she was fixing my hem. But when Mama wasn't looking, I hunched my back so I'd look smaller.

At school, I struggled mightily to fit my long legs under my desk. So Papa built a big desk for me. He brought it to school in a wagon pulled by horses.

"Stand straight, Ella Kate, and show off your new desk," Papa said with pride. I guess he couldn't see how mortified I was. No other girl in my school needed a special desk or wore shoes as big as her pa's—men's size twelve.

My best friend was a girl named Pearl. Just like her name, Pearl was small and beautiful. When I got teased at recess on account of my size, Pearl suggested we run away.

"We'll hide you in a secret place where no one can find you," Pearl said. She was only trying to be nice. But where could I hide? I was too big for everything.

I was too big for the world.

When I was thirteen, I stood almost six feet tall.

My classmates chose me to recite the Declaration of Independence at a big Fourth of July celebration. I was surprised and honored. People from three counties would be there!

I practiced for weeks. When it was time, I walked out on stage and began to recite the famous words. But I stopped cold when I heard voices from the crowd.

"Would you look at that girl?" cried one man. "She's as tall as a barn!"

"Her hands are as big as skillets," laughed a woman.

"I'll tell you what that girl is," yelled a boy. "She's a freak!"

I ran off the stage in tears.

Mama was upset too, but she waited to cry until I'd gone to bed. "Don't worry," Papa said. "No one's ever treating Ella Kate that way again. We'll keep her safe inside this house for as long as she lives."

From my bed I listened, wishing I could climb inside the big
night sky and hide there forever.

But I kept growing.

By the age of sixteen, I was seven feet tall. At seventeen I was a foot taller.

One day a man visited our farm. He managed a museum in Chicago.

"I hear you have a daughter who stands eight feet tall," the man said. "My customers would pay good money to see that. And I'd gladly pay Miss Ella Kate for her time."

Papa got mad. "Nobody's paying money to gawk at our girl!" he fumed.

But something in me trusted the man.

"I believe I'll take that job," I said.

And so when I was eighteen, my parents and I boarded the train
to Chicago.

For one month, I wore a long dress and a serious expression for seven hours a day while people stared at me.

I made one thousand dollars, which was a whole lot of money in 1890. Back then you could buy twelve pencils and a bottle of ink for a dime.

The following year, I received a letter from the man in Chicago, asking me to return to his museum. This time, he wanted me to come for five months. He offered to pay me five thousand dollars.

"Five *months*?" Papa protested. "That's too long."

"I don't mind," I said. "Mama can come with me. Besides, five thousand dollars is nothing to sneeze at, Papa. It's more than you can make in five years of farming."

This was true and Papa knew it. He laughed. I was becoming better at business than he was!

WORLD'S COLUMBIAN EXHIBITION 1893

BARNUM & BAILEY GREATEST SHOW ON EARTH

1897

TALLEST WOMAN ON EARTH!

I returned to Chicago in 1891, and for the next six years, I traveled the country. I appeared in museums, exhibitions, traveling circus shows, and even a world's fair.

People paid ten cents to see me stand in my fancy dresses. You couldn't blame folks for staring. After all, when I finally stopped growing at the age of twenty-two, I stood a towering eight feet, four inches tall in my size twenty-four shoes.

My hands were also impressive. Once, I removed a ring from my finger and gave it to a baby to wear as a bracelet. It fit perfectly.

Other times I held a one-thousand-dollar bill in my hand. Anyone who could reach the money unassisted was welcome to take it. No one ever did.

After I had made enough
money, I went back to
Rainbow. The first thing
I did was visit the bank
that had lent Papa
money to buy our farm.
I paid off the debt. I
figured it was the least
I could do to thank Papa
and Mama for all they'd
done for me.

Then I did something
for myself.

I bought some land and started building a house. I paid
workers with my own money and told them to build my house
with tall ceilings and high windows. I ordered custom-built
furniture.

Finally I had a house in which I could stand up straight
without stooping. I had the longest bed in town. I even
ordered a custom-made buggy and bought a strong horse to
pull it.

Friends and neighbors liked to visit me at my new house. They always asked to hear about my travels. I told them about the big cities and new-fangled automobiles I'd seen. I described the mountains and oceans. I even imitated the tigers and elephants that appeared with me in the circus. Most of my friends had never left home or seen such things.

But the more I talked about my travels, the more I missed them.

So the year after I finished my house, I returned to work.
I enjoyed my days as a circus show star.
Sometimes my unusual size came in handy. When I was
introduced to Mr. Charles Ringling at a dinner party in 1907,

I was able to shake his hand without moving from my place at the end of the table. My friend Little Lord Robert thought that was a fine and dandy trick.

Another time when a bellboy brought ice water to my hotel room, instead of opening the door, I reached through the transom and retrieved the pitcher from his hands. I hope I didn't give him too much of a fright!

I always tried to be respectful. And I found that most people were respectful in return.

Of course there was always one person in every crowd who couldn't resist making a cruel joke about my appearance. More than one rude spectator stuck my leg with a pin to see if I stood on stilts.

When that happened, I just whispered to myself what Mama and Papa always told me when I was growing up: "Stand straight, Ella Kate." The more I said it, the better I felt.

And the more I saw of the world, the more I wanted to see. Because as big as I was, the world was so much bigger.

And I intended to see it all.

A NOTE FROM THE AUTHOR

Ella Ewing (left) with her traveling companion, Maude Wilson, ca. 1907 (Circus World Museum, Baraboo, Wisconsin)

Ella's condition, known today as gigantism, was poorly understood by doctors of the day, who didn't know how to treat the gland disorder. After she began to grow at an abnormal rate, Ella suffered serious emotional distress. By all accounts, she was a shy, sensitive girl who disliked the attention her unusual appearance attracted. But as she grew older, Ella discovered that the very thing that made her cry as a child also made it possible for her to lead a remarkable life.

For almost twenty years, Ella toured the United States and Canada as a star attraction in the biggest traveling shows of the day. Her size allowed her to witness many of the great events of the late nineteenth and early twentieth centuries.

At a time when most people traveled very little and women did not enjoy even the right to vote, Ella was both famous and financially independent. Between tours, she always returned home and shared her experiences with friends who could only dream of seeing the things Ella had seen. Ella's house became the social center of her county.

Ella Ewing never married or had children. She died in 1913 at the age of forty. Her house burned to the ground in 1967. By then, even Rainbow, Missouri, had disappeared from the map.

Fortunately, those who knew Ella found a fitting way to remember her. Not far from the home Ella built in Scotland County, Missouri, rests the Ella Ewing Lake. Dedicated in 1969, the large, reflective body of water is an appropriate tribute to the quiet woman still known in Missouri as the Gentle Giantess.

ELLA'S bureau: 6' tall

Circumference of ELLA'S head: 26"

ELLA'S glove size 24

ACTUAL SIZE